39026

The Blackfeet

People of the Dark Moccasins

by **Karen Bush Gibson**

Consultant:
Gregory R. Campbell, Professor
Department of Anthropology
University of Montana
Missoula, Montana

978
Gib

Bridgestone Books

an imprint of Capstone Press
Mankato, Minnesota

Bridgestone Books are published by Capstone Press
151 Good Counsel Drive, P.O. Box 669, Mankato, Minnesota 56002
http://www.capstone-press.com

Library of Congress Cataloging-in-Publication Data
Gibson, Karen Bush.
    The Blackfeet: People of the dark moccasins/by Karen Bush Gibson.
        p. cm. — (American Indian nations series)
    Includes bibliographical references and index.
    Summary: An overview of the past and present of the Blackfeet people.
Traces their customs, family life, history, and culture, as well as relations with the
U.S. government.
    ISBN 0-7368-1565-1 (hardcover)
    1. Siksika Indians—Juvenile literature. 2. Piegan Indians—Juvenile literature. 3.
Kainah Indians—Juvenile literature. [1. Siksika Indians. 2. Piegan Indians. 3. Kainah
Indians. 4. Indians of North America—Great Plains.] I. Title. II. Series.
E99.S54 G53 2003
978'.004973—dc21   2002012000

Editorial Credits
Charles Pederson, editor; Kia Adams, designer; Alta Schaffer, photo researcher;
Karen Risch, product planning editor

Photo Credits
Angelika Harden-Norman, 9, 32, 34
Art Resource/Smithsonian Institution, 20
Blackfeet Nation/Chief Earl Old Person, 37
Capstone Press/Gary Sundermeyer, 13; Cherokee, N.C., 28–29
Corbis, 30–31, 38–39; Philip Gendreau, 14; Werner Forman, 18, 44; Hulton
    Deutsch Collection, 26; Stapleton Collection, 31; Corbis/Historical Picture
    Archive, 25
Kit Breen, 40, 45
Marilyn "Angel" Wynn, cover (inset) , 4, 16, 43
North Wind Picture Archives, 22
Stock Montage, Inc., 12; The Newbery Library, cover (main), 10

1 2 3 4 5 6 08 07 06 05 04 03

Table of Contents

1 Who Are the Blackfeet? 5
2 Traditional Life. 11
3 U.S. Expansion Brings Change 23
4 The Blackfeet Today 33
5 Sharing the Traditions. 39

Features

Map: The Blackfeet Past and Present 7
Recipe: Pemmican 13
Blackfeet Timeline 44
Glossary. 46
Internet Sites 46
Places to Write and Visit. 47
For Further Reading 47
Index 48

Modern Blackfeet participate in drumming and other traditional activities. The Blackfeet live in Alberta and Saskatchewan in Canada, and Montana in the United States.

Chapter One

Who Are the Blackfeet?

The Blackfeet people are an American
Indian nation who have lived in the
Great Plains of North America since
about the 1700s. The Great Plains are a
flat grassland stretching from the
Mississippi River west to the Rocky
Mountains. The Blackfeet originally lived
in the northeast. Many Blackfeet moved
west and today live in Montana and
the Canadian provinces of Alberta
and Saskatchewan.

The 2000 U.S. Census shows that
27,104 people in the United States

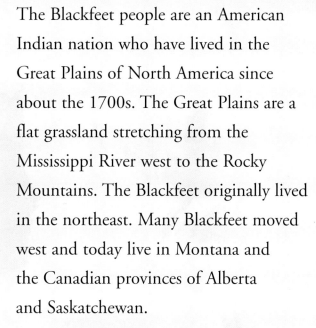

consider themselves Blackfeet. The Blackfeet have one of the 10 largest American Indian populations in the United States.

The Blackfeet living in the United States are part of the Blackfeet Confederacy. A confederacy is a group of bands or tribes who have joined together to help each other.

Four separate nations make up the Blackfeet Confederacy. The Blackfeet Nation is in Montana. The Piegan, the Siksika, or Northern Piegan, and the Kainai, or Blood, make their home in Canada. The four tribes sometimes are called the Blackfoot Confederacy instead of the Blackfeet Confederacy. The tribes have separate governments but still regularly come together as a nation for religious and social celebrations.

Canadian reservations called reserves are home to the Piegan, the Siksika, and the Kainai. The only part of the confederacy inside the United States is the Blackfeet Nation of Montana. These Blackfeet sometimes are called the Pikuni or Piegan. This group lives on the Blackfeet Reservation. The reservation headquarters is located in Browning, in northwestern Montana.

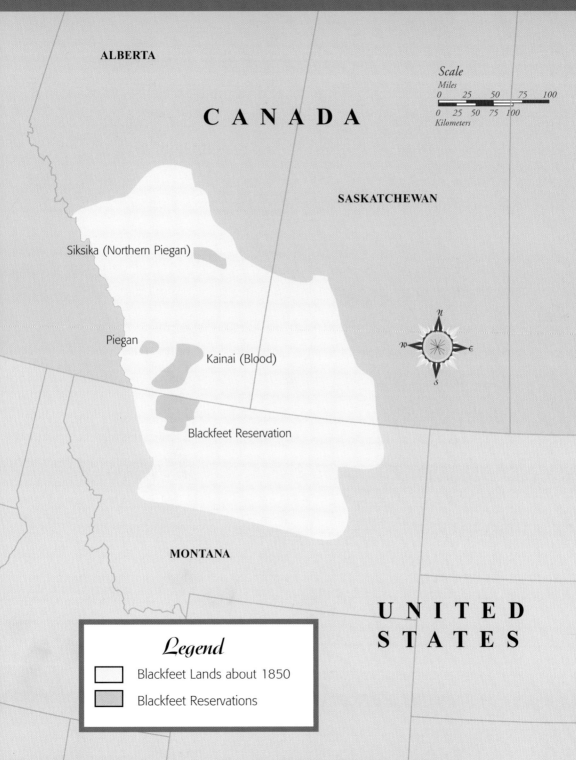

ALBERTA

CANADA

SASKATCHEWAN

Scale

Miles

0   25   50   75   100

0   25 50 75 100

Kilometers

Siksika (Northern Piegan)

Piegan

Kainai (Blood)

Blackfeet Reservation

MONTANA

UNITED STATES

Legend

Blackfeet Lands about 1850

Blackfeet Reservations

The name Blackfeet probably came from the color on the bottom of the people's leather shoes. In the past, the Blackfeet dyed or painted the bottoms of these moccasins black. One story tells of Blackfeet walking through the ashes of prairie fires, which turned their moccasins black. Another name for the Blackfeet is Lords of the Plains. At one time, they were one of the most powerful Indian nations on the Great Plains.

The Blackfeet adapted to the harsh winters of the nearly treeless northern Great Plains. Only an occasional dip in the land or a flat-topped hill helped block the wind. Food was hard to find in winter because of the weather. During summer and autumn, the Blackfeet people gathered and prepared food for use during winter.

The people of the Blackfeet Confederacy share a respect for their history and culture. They celebrate their heritage through the Sun Dance, a religious ceremony of many Plains tribes, and other gatherings.

Tepees and other shelters helped the Blackfeet survive harsh winters on the Great Plains.

The Blackfeet used horses to pull their belongings on a sled called a travois.

Chapter Two

Traditional Life

The Blackfeet people once lived in the forests of what later became the northeast United States. By 1600, the Blackfeet had moved north of the Great Lakes into present-day Canada. The area they moved to had forests filled with game animals for hunting.

Battles with neighboring tribes led the Blackfeet to move from this wooded Great Lakes area. They packed their belongings on A-shaped sleds designed for dry land. The sleds were called travois. The Blackfeet did not have horses before the 1700s, so until then, dogs pulled the Blackfeet travois.

The Blackfeet moved from the eastern woodlands west to the Great Plains. Their territory on the Great Plains ranged from the Saskatchewan River in Canada to the Missouri River in Montana.

The Importance of Buffalo

On the plains, the Blackfeet found herds of animals called buffalo. Blackfeet hunted buffalo in several ways. Most commonly, they used a buffalo jump. Hunters frightened a herd of buffalo into running over a cliff. The hunters could then kill as many buffalo as they needed. Using another method, a hunter disguised himself with the skin and horns of a buffalo. When the hunter was close enough, he shot a buffalo with an arrow or speared it with a lance.

The Blackfeet hunted buffalo to provide food for themselves and their families.

Pemmican

The Blackfeet made pemmican to eat during the winter and while traveling. They cut buffalo meat into thin strips, dried the meat, then crushed it into powder. They mixed berries and buffalo fat with the meat powder to form patties. These patties fit easily into leather pouches for travel. The modern version of pemmican below is made with dried fruit and beef jerky.

Ingredients

2 ounces (55 grams) dried beef jerky
4 dried apple slices
1 cup (240 mL) raisins or dried cherries

Equipment

dry-ingredient measuring cups
blender or food processor
2 sheets wax paper
fork

rolling pin
pie pan
pot holders

What You Do

1. Finely chop the dried beef jerky in a blender or food processor.
2. Add the apples and the dried fruit to the beef in the blender. Grind until finely chopped.
3. Place beef and fruit mixture between two sheets of wax paper. Use a rolling pin to roll over the top sheet until mixture is approximately ⅛ inch (3 millimeters) thick.
4. To dry in sun, place mixture and wax paper in sunny spot for up to two days. To dry in oven, remove pemmican from wax paper, place in a pie pan, and bake at 350°F (180°C) for two hours. Using a fork, turn pemmican several times during baking.
5. When cool and completely dry, break off pieces to eat.

Serves 3 to 4

The Blackfeet used buffalo meat in different ways. It could be boiled, roasted, or dried. Hunters could mix the meat with fat and berries to make a food called pemmican. Because this food lasted a long time without spoiling, it could be stored for winter or travel. Hunters often ate the buffalo heart meat minutes after killing a buffalo. They considered it delicious.

Buffalo were used for more than food. Buffalo skins provided covering for a type of tent called a tepee. The Blackfeet made robes and moccasins of buffalo skins to use during the winter. Blackfeet soap came from buffalo fat. The Blackfeet carved eating utensils, sewing needles, and tools

For hundreds of years, horses have been important to the Blackfeet. The Blackfeet first saw horses in the early 1700s.

Tepees

Traditional Blackfeet people followed the buffalo, so the Blackfeet had to be ready to move quickly. Their tentlike homes called tepees allowed them to do that. Tepees were made of buffalo hides sewn together and draped over a frame of long, straight poles. Tepees were warm in the winter and cool in the summer. Tepees made a good home for moving camp quickly. They were sturdy and could stand up to strong winds. Yet, they were easy to take apart for packing.

Once a woman took down a tepee, she used its poles to make a travois. The woman then packed the tepee and other family belongings onto the travois.

Using paints made from plants and other natural ingredients, the Blackfeet often painted their tepees. Sometimes, the paintings told a story. Other times, they were simple designs.

from buffalo bones. The buffalo stomach and bladder made good containers for liquids. The Blackfeet even used dried buffalo manure as fuel for fires.

The Importance of Horses

Around 1730, the Blackfeet saw horses for the first time. The horses the Blackfeet saw belonged to an American Indian nation called the Shoshone. The Shoshone had gained horses many years earlier. The Blackfeet called horses "ponokamita,"

Quillwork

Winters were a time for the Blackfeet to stay near home because game animals were scarce. Instead of hunting, people often stayed warm by sitting near fires inside their tepees. To pass the time, they told stories while decorating animal skins used for clothing, bags, and tepees. One of the decorating methods was called quillwork.

Quillwork involved using sharp porcupine spines colored with dyes made from plants. After the dye dried on these porcupine quills, the women sewed the quills into clothing and moccasins. Soaking the quills in water softened them. The women then could flatten the quills and more easily bend them to create designs. The leather bag pictured at right is decorated with different-colored quills.

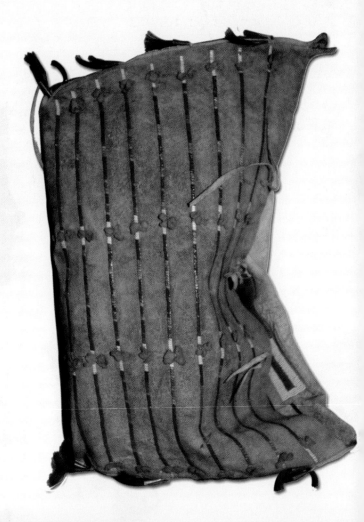

which means elk dogs. The Blackfeet began to trade items for horses and soon became expert riders.

Hunting became easier. Hunters did not have to sneak up on or run after buffalo. Instead, horses allowed hunters to race alongside the buffalo, riding with their feet hooked around the horse. Horseback hunters more easily chased and killed elk, deer, moose, sheep, and other game animals for food.

Family Life

Blackfeet tribes normally split into bands of about 20 to 30 people for traveling. The bands came together at various times for celebrations.

The bands prized leadership skills and chose their chiefs wisely. A war chief who had shown bravery in battle led a band in wartime. A peace chief who was a good speaker led during times of peace.

Boys and girls prepared to take adult roles in their bands. They learned to ride horses at an early age. Boys played with toy bows and arrows until they learned to hunt. Many girls enjoyed playing with dolls with hair made from buffalo hair. This play helped girls learn to care for children.

Girls and boys had more responsibilities as they grew older. Girls learned to cook. They learned to prepare buffalo hides as leather. They also gathered wild plants and berries for food. Boys began to provide food for the village by hunting.

Women and men wore different kinds of clothing. Women wore long leather dresses made from the skins of antelope or mountain sheep. Men wore leggings and shirts of leather. The Blackfeet often decorated their clothing with paint, leather fringe, porcupine quills, or dyes.

Blackfeet marriage was not complicated. Adult Blackfeet men chose their marriage partners. To receive permission to

The Blackfeet often decorated their leather clothing with fringe.

marry, a man showed a woman's father his skills as a hunter or warrior. If the woman's father agreed to the marriage, the man and woman exchanged gifts of horses or clothes. They then were considered married. A married couple lived in their own tepee or with the husband's family. Sometimes, a man married more than one wife. When he did, he often married sisters.

Blackfeet Societies

The Blackfeet had societies within the nation. Men, women, warriors, and spiritual people belonged to these groups. Each person had to be invited to join one of the groups.

Before receiving an invitation to a society, a young man performed a vision quest. The man began this event by spiritually cleansing himself in a sweat lodge. He then went off alone for four days of fasting and prayer. He hoped for a dreamlike vision to explain his future. After having a vision, he returned to the village and was ready to join a society.

Men in warrior societies fought for their people. To prepare for battle, a warrior cleansed himself by sweating in a sweat lodge. He then painted his body and sometimes his horse for battle. Leaders of warrior societies carried a spear or lance called a coup stick. They decorated the stick with feathers, skins, and other tokens. Some warriors wore a type of long leather belt. They staked this belt into the ground and fought their enemies to show their bravery.

Religious societies had several duties. They protected holy Blackfeet items. They led ceremonies to protect warriors before battle. The holiest ceremony was the Sun Dance, or Medicine Lodge Ceremony. The Blackfeet believed this summer ceremony carried prayers to the Creator. They

About 1920, artist Joseph Henry Sharp created this painting called *Sweetgrass Medicine Ceremony*. Religious ceremonies always have been important in everyday Blackfeet life.

Brown Weasel

As a girl, Brown Weasel learned everything a Blackfeet girl must know. She also wanted to know what her brothers learned. She wanted to ride horses and hunt with a bow and arrows. Her father taught her these skills and began taking her on buffalo hunts.

During one hunt, enemy warriors attacked Brown Weasel and her father. They shot her father's horse. Brown Weasel leaned far over the side of her horse as she had seen Blackfeet warriors do. She pulled her father up behind her and safely escaped.

After her parents died, Brown Weasel began to follow war groups out of camp, though she was not allowed to fight. One night, she saw two enemy warriors trying to steal Blackfeet horses. She killed one of the enemies and claimed his horse as her own.

After this and other acts of bravery, the village leaders allowed Brown Weasel to perform a vision quest. She went alone from her village for four days. During her quest, she had a vision that told her to live her life for the sun and her people. After successfully completing her vision quest, she was allowed to dress as a warrior. She also received a new name, Running Eagle. She was a brave Blackfeet warrior for many years before dying in battle. She received a warrior's funeral.

believed that the prayers assured the well-being of the Blackfeet and the continued presence of many buffalo.

Women's societies had a variety of duties. Groups of women might be responsible for creating quillwork, helping warriors prepare for battle, or performing ceremonies to help hunters.

Beginning in 1804, Lewis and Clark, center, led an expedition to explore the West. In 1806, they met the Blackfeet and other American Indians and tried to become friends with them.

Chapter Three

U.S. Expansion Brings Change

In 1806, the Blackfeet had their first known meeting with white people. Meriwether Lewis and William Clark led a group of explorers. They were mapping the Missouri River for the U.S. government. Blackfeet warriors met some men who had left the main exploring group. Lewis led this smaller group. He explained to the Blackfeet that the United States wanted peace with all Indian nations.

The Blackfeet knew the group had traded guns to their enemies, the Shoshone and Nez Perce peoples. The Blackfeet worried that their enemies had such powerful weapons. The Blackfeet tried to take guns from Lewis and his men. Lewis' men killed two Blackfeet warriors and drove away the others. The Blackfeet did not get guns that day.

More Contact with White People

During the next 10 years, the Blackfeet began to trade with British traders in Canada. They traded animal skins for British guns and bullets. More trappers and traders arrived in Blackfeet land. The Blackfeet traded for beads, blankets, horses, and guns at posts along the Missouri River.

In the 1830s, other white people became interested in the Blackfeet. During the winter of 1833, German explorer Prince Maxmillian and Swiss painter Karl Bodmer spent a month with the Blackfeet. Maxmillian was the first European to observe the men's societies of the Blackfeet. Bodmer painted scenes of Blackfeet life.

Contact with white traders brought diseases to the Blackfeet. In 1836, four outbreaks of smallpox struck and killed many Blackfeet. Smallpox was a deadly disease carried by Europeans and Americans. About half the nearly 5,000 Blackfeet died in these first outbreaks. In 1845 and 1869, outbreaks of smallpox and other diseases killed even more Blackfeet.

Karl Bodmer painted many scenes of Blackfeet life. The painting above shows a Blackfeet camp in the 1830s.

Warrior Headdresses

The headdress is a powerful Blackfeet symbol. The original headdress was called a stand-up headdress. It was one of the few American Indian headdresses where the feathers stood up straight. The Blackfeet believed this stand-up headdress was magical. Only great warriors could wear it. The Blackfeet hid the headdress after 1898, when the U.S. government made it against the law for the Blackfeet to take part in their traditional ceremonies.

Another Blackfeet headdress was the Sioux-style eagle feather headdress like the one pictured below. This type of headdress swept back to the shoulders. Blackfeet leaders who visited Washington, D.C., to meet with government officials often wore this kind of headdress.

Mountain Chief, Bird Rattler, Turtle, Little Blaze, Curly Bear, and other Blackfeet leaders wore warrior headdresses into the early 1900s. Today, the Blackfeet consider headdresses sacred. Only a few honored leaders may wear them.

Hunger

During the mid-1800s, white hunters hunted the buffalo until they were almost gone. Without buffalo, the Blackfeet could not get enough food for themselves. They had to depend on the U.S. government for food. In 1855, Blackfeet leader Lame Bull made a peace agreement with the government. The Lame Bull Treaty promised the Blackfeet $20,000 in goods and services in exchange for the Blackfeet moving onto a reservation.

By 1860, few buffalo were left. The cattle of white ranchers on Blackfeet land ate the grass that the buffalo needed. The Blackfeet could no longer get food and shelter from the buffalo. The Blackfeet depended on supplies promised in treaties. Government food took a long time to arrive. When it did, the food was often rotten.

Hungry Blackfeet raided white settlements for food and supplies, causing trouble with the U.S. Army. In January 1870, the army attacked 219 peaceful Blackfeet in a village on the Marias River in present-day Montana. The attack was in revenge for an earlier Blackfeet raid. At the end of the fighting, only 46 villagers remained alive.

The Blackfeet called the winter of 1883–1884 Starvation Winter. No government supplies came, and the Blackfeet had no buffalo to hunt. That winter, more than 600 Blackfeet died of hunger.

Effects of U.S. Laws

In 1874, the U.S. government voted to change Blackfeet reservation borders. They did not discuss this change with the Blackfeet. The new borders reduced the amount of Blackfeet land. The Blackfeet received no money for the land they lost. The Kainai, Siksika, and Piegan bands moved to Canada. They settled on reserves, leaving only the Pikuni Blackfeet in U.S. territory.

Indian children at boarding schools were not allowed to speak their language or practice their customs. The children pictured here attended school in North Carolina.

In 1898, the U.S. Congress passed the Curtis Act. This law strengthened an 1883 law that got rid of tribal governments. The earlier law also made it illegal to practice traditional Indian religions. These laws were meant to force Indians to become more like white people.

Blackfeet children were sent to government and church boarding schools. Students at these live-in schools were not allowed to speak their native language, practice their customs, or wear traditional clothing.

In 1907, the U.S. government adopted a policy of allotment on the Blackfeet Reservation. The law said that families must live separately on their own land, not in a larger tribal group. Each Blackfeet family received a 160-acre

(65-hectare) farm. After the Blackfeet moved to their farms, much land was left that no longer belonged to the Blackfeet. The government kept the extra land or sold it to white settlers.

The 1910 U.S. Census reported 2,268 people living on the Blackfeet Reservation in Montana. This population was less than half the number who had lived in that area at the time of Lewis and Clark's journey in 1804.

In 1919, a drought destroyed crops and raised the price of beef. This lack of food caused hunger among the Blackfeet and further reduced their population. Many Blackfeet and other Indians were forced to sell their allotted land to pay for taxes the government said they owed.

In 1934, the Indian Reorganization Act ended allotments. This law allowed tribes to choose their own governments and again openly practice their culture.

In 1935, the Blackfeet Nation of Montana began a Tribal Business Council. The nation also adopted a constitution. Since that time, the Blackfeet Nation has had its own government.

The two men shown above lived on the Blackfeet Reservation at the time of the 1910 census. The census reported 2,268 people on the reservation at that time.

Statues of Blackfeet warriors on horseback stand at the entrance to the Blackfeet Reservation in Browning, Montana.

Chapter Four

The Blackfeet Today

Today, more than 30,000 people belong to the Blackfeet Confederacy. Many live on reserves in Canada. About 8,500 Blackfeet live on their Montana reservation of 1.5 million acres (610,000 hectares).

The Blackfeet Reservation in Montana is east of Glacier National Park. At one time, the Blackfeet controlled the land that makes up the park. They sold a large portion of it to the U.S. government as part of an 1896 agreement. Americans had hoped to discover copper or gold on the land but found nothing. In 1910, the area became Glacier National Park. Today, some Blackfeet work at the park. The Blackfeet sometimes hold ceremonies at sacred areas inside the park. Tourists visiting Glacier National Park often travel through the Blackfeet Reservation.

The Blackfeet consider the education of their children very important. The students above are learning traditional Blackfeet drumming.

Earning Money

Unemployment is high on the Blackfeet Reservation. Many people work as farmers or ranchers, but not enough of these nearby jobs are available. To find better jobs, many Blackfeet today live in towns and cities instead of on reservations.

Some companies off the reservation pay the Blackfeet for the use of oil, natural gas, and other resources on reservation land. The Blackfeet operate other businesses, such as the Blackfeet Writing Company, which opened in 1972.

To earn money for the entire Blackfeet Nation, the Blackfeet Tribal Business Council runs museums, gift shops, and rodeos for tourists. In Canada, the Northern Piegan make clothing and moccasins. The Kainai operate a shopping center and factory.

Education

Education is important to the Blackfeet. The Blackfeet Community College is a two-year college in Browning, Montana, the Blackfeet tribal headquarters. The Blackfeet Tribal Council started the college in 1974.

Many Blackfeet educational efforts have been successful. In 1979, the Montana state government began to require all public school teachers on or near reservations to have a background in American Indian studies. This law has helped non-Blackfeet people increase their understanding of the Blackfeet culture. In 1989, the Siksika of Canada established a high school to go with an elementary school already on their reserve.

The Blackfeet Nation

A tribal council governs each group within the Blackfeet Confederacy. A chairperson or head chief leads the council. In Montana, the council has eight members and a chairperson. Each council member serves a two-year or four-year term. A tribal chief leads ceremonies.

A blue tribal flag represents the Blackfeet Nation in Montana. It shows a spear called a ceremonial lance. The lance has 29 feathers on the left side. A center ring of 32 white and black eagle feathers surrounds a map of the Blackfeet Reservation. On the map are a warrior headdress and the words "the Blackfeet Nation" and "Pikuni."

Earl Old Person

Chief Earl Old Person was born on April 13, 1929, to Juniper and Molly Old Person. He was educated at reservation schools in Montana.

Chief Old Person has worked most of his life for the good of the Blackfeet people. At about age 7, he began to perform traditional Blackfeet songs and dances throughout Montana. In 1972, he founded a pen and pencil company called the Blackfeet Writing Company. Today, the company is one of the reservation's largest employers.

In 1978, Earl Old Person was appointed chief of the Blackfeet. He has served as the chairperson of the Tribal Business Council. He was the youngest member of the council and has served for more than 40 years.

Chief Old Person has worked hard to establish tribal programs to help the Blackfeet. Alcoholism prevention is important to the chief. He also has argued for Indian voting rights and greater tribal independence.

Chief Old Person has received many honors for his work. The American Civil Liberties Union (ACLU) and U.S. presidents from Eisenhower to Clinton have honored him. Chief Old Person also has received honors from Canadian prime ministers and the royal family of England.

In 1916, Frances Densmore, left, recorded a Blackfeet man speaking his language. The Blackfeet wanted to preserve their language for their children to learn.

Sharing the Traditions

The Blackfeet continue many of their cultural traditions. They want their children to know the Pikuni language and other traditional knowledge. In the early 1900s, Frances Densmore was one white person who helped record the Blackfeet language.

By the 1950s and 1960s, few people still spoke Pikuni as a native language. Blackfeet leaders asked for help from older Pikuni speakers. During the 1970s, some Blackfeet became concerned about the state of their language. These elders have succeeded in helping many Blackfeet learn

A Blackfeet dancer carries an eagle staff at a powwow. Powwows and other celebrations and ceremonies help the Blackfeet honor their culture.

their traditional language. Today, many Blackfeet learn Pikuni in school. Some children learn the language at home from parents or grandparents.

In 1994, the Blackfeet Confederacy accepted Pikuni as the official Blackfeet language. Many Blackfeet on reservations and reserves speak both Pikuni and English.

Along with teaching their language, the Blackfeet have restarted societies like the Black Lodge Society. This society is responsible for protecting the songs and dances of the Blackfeet. Such societies keep Blackfeet traditions alive.

Ceremonies help the Blackfeet respect and share their culture. Religious leaders lead today's ceremonies. They hold an eagle staff decorated with designs, feathers, and the head of an eagle.

The Blackfeet announce the coming of spring with the opening of five medicine bundles. One bundle is opened at the first sound of thunder in the spring. Each time the thunders rolls, another bundle is opened, until all five are opened. In this way, the Blackfeet welcome spring.

One of the biggest celebrations held annually is a powwow called North American Indian Days. During the second week in July, the Blackfeet and members of other Indian nations from all over North America gather on the Blackfeet Reservation in Browning, Montana. The gathering takes place at a traditional camp with painted tepees. It is the largest celebration of its kind on the continent. North American Indian Days is open to the public. The Blackfeet encourage visitors to attend. The gathering lasts four days, the time needed for vision quests.

Another annual celebration is the Sun Dance. From the late 1890s until 1934, the Sun Dance was illegal. The Blackfeet held the Sun Dance secretly. After 1934, the ceremony was legal, and the Blackfeet again could openly perform it. Today, the eight-day event occurs each summer. Prayers, dancing, singing, and offerings honor the Creator. The Sun Dance provides a chance for Blackfeet to share news and visit with each other.

The Blackfeet have worked to preserve their culture and pass on their traditions. They want their children to know what it means to be Blackfeet. They want their children to be proud of their Blackfeet heritage.

Hand drummers perform a traditional Blackfeet musical style.

Blackfeet Timeline

Blackfeet meet members of Lewis and Clark's expedition.

The Siksika, Piegan, and Kainai bands move to Canada.

The United States adopts the policy of allotment.

| 1730 | 1806 | 1874 | 1883–1884 | 1907 |

Blackfeet see horses for the first time.

More than 600 Blackfeet die of hunger during Starvation Winter.

Blackfeet warriors sometimes carried coup sticks like this.

Congress passes
the Indian
Reorganization Act.

The Blackfeet Writing
Company begins
operating on the
Blackfeet Reservation.

1934   **1935**   **1972**   **1994**

The Blackfeet Confederacy
adopts Pikuni as the
official Blackfeet language.

The Blackfeet Tribal
Business Council forms.

Glossary

ceremony (SER-uh-moh-nee)—formal actions, words, or music that honor a person or an event

confederacy (kuhn-FED-ur-uh-see)—a union of people or tribes with a common goal

moccasin (MOK-uh-suhn)—a soft leather shoe

pemmican (PEM-uh-kuhn)—a mixture of dried buffalo meat, berries, and fat

quill (KWIL)—a long, pointed spine of a porcupine

reservation (rez-ur-VAY-shuhn)—an area of land that the U.S. government sets aside for an American Indian tribe to use

travois (truh-VOY)—an A-shaped frame of two tepee poles dragged behind a horse or dog

Internet Sites

Track down many sites about the Blackfeet. Visit the FACT HOUND at *http://www.facthound.com*. IT IS EASY! IT IS FUN!

1) Go to *http://www.facthound.com*
2) Type in: 0736815651
3) Click on "FETCH IT!" and FACT HOUND will find several links hand-picked by our editors.

Relax and let our pal FACT HOUND do the research for you!

Places to Write and Visit

The Blackfeet Tribal Business Council
P.O. Box 850
Browning, MT 59417

Museum of the Plains Indian
P.O. Box 410
Browning, MT 59417

The Piegan Institute
P.O. Box 909
Browning, MT 59417

Siksika Nation
P.O. Box 1100
Siksika, AB T0J 3W0
Canada

For Further Reading

Bial, Raymond. *The Blackfeet.* Lifeways. New York: Benchmark Books, 2003.

Sharp, Anne Wallace. *The Blackfeet.* Indigenous Peoples of North America. San Diego: Lucent Books, 2002.

Wood-Trost, Lucille. *Native Americans of the Plains.* Indigenous Peoples of North America. San Diego: Lucent Books, 2000.

Index

allotment, 29, 30

Blackfeet Community College, 35
Blackfeet Confederacy, 6, 33, 36
Blackfeet government, 6, 29,
   30–31
Blackfeet Writing Company,
   35, 37
Blackfoot, 6
Bodmer, Karl, 24, 25
Brown Weasel, 21
Browning, Montana, 6, 32, 35, 42
buffalo, 12, 13, 14, 15, 17, 21
   disappearance of, 27, 28

Canada, 4, 6, 12, 24, 28, 33,
   35, 36
ceremonies, 8, 20, 21, 26, 34, 36,
   40, 41
   Sun Dance, 8, 20–21, 42
chief, 17, 36, 37
climate, 8, 9, 15, 41
clothing, 8, 14, 16, 18, 26, 29
Curtis Act, 29

disease, 24

education, 28, 29, 34, 35–36,
   37, 41
employment, 34, 35, 37

family life, 17–18
female roles, 15, 16, 17–18, 21
flag, 36
food, 8, 12, 14, 17
   lack of, 27–28, 30
   pemmican, 13, 14

Glacier National Park, 33, 34
Great Plains, 5, 8, 9, 11

headdress, 26, 36
horse, 10, 11, 14, 15, 17, 19, 21,
   24, 32
hunting, 11, 12, 16, 17, 21, 28

Indian Reorganization Act, 30

Kainai, 6, 28, 35

language, 28, 29, 38, 39, 41
Lewis and Clark, 22, 23, 24, 30

male roles, 17, 19, 21
marriage, 18–19
medicine bundle, 41
Medicine Lodge Ceremony,
   20–21
migration, 5, 11–12, 15, 17, 28
Missouri River, 12, 23, 24

North American Indian Days, 42
Northern Piegan, 6, 35

Old Person, Chief Earl, 37

Piegan, 6
Pikuni, 28, 39, 41
population, 5–6, 28, 30, 31, 33

quillwork, 16, 21

religion, 6, 8, 20–21, 29, 41
Rocky Mountains, 5

shelter, 9, 14, 15, 16, 19, 27, 42
Shoshone, 15, 23
Siksika, 6, 28, 36
societies, 19–21, 24, 41
Starvation Winter, 28

trade, 17, 18, 23, 24
travois, 10, 11, 15
treaties, 27
Tribal Business Council, 31, 35, 37

U.S. Army, 27
U.S. Census, 5, 30, 31
U.S. government, 23, 26, 27, 28,
   29, 33

vision quest, 19, 21, 42

war, 11, 17, 19, 20, 21